In loving memory of Luke

Away in the countryside
Over the hills and then
Inside a little forest
You'll find a little den.

And that's where the fox lives
With his tail of bushy red
The den inside the forest
Is the fox's little bed

01

This fox was so lovely
As red as red can be
"But being a fox is dull"
"It's not the life for me!"

02

I wish that I was big
I wish that I was strong
I wish that I was grey
And that my snout was long

My tail is too bushy
And my fur is too red
The wolves are big and strong
But I'm so small instead"

04

I wish I was a wolf!
I wish that I could prowl
That I could join the wolves
Out on their nightly howl

yowl

The fox was oh so sad.
When he heard the wolves howl
The only sound he could make
Was a pathetic yowl

And then, one starry night
The fox had such a fright
While he was watching wolves
There came a big bright light

"So you want to be a wolf?"
The little green light said
"Who's there?" The fox was scared
"How are you in my head?"

08

"I am Jinx the Fairy,
And I have heard your cry
I would like to help you
At least I'd like to try!"

Now the fox could see her
Her dress of emerald green
A light shining behind
This little fairy queen

"I can make you a wolf
As easy as can be
I can make you a wolf
Just like you want to be!"

"Oh yes please!" the fox said
His wish was coming true
He would become a wolf
And do what all wolves do!"

"I'll say some magic words
I'll cast a fairy spell
Throw in a bit of dust
Some glowing gems as well

As the magic happens
It might feel a bit strange
When your body transforms
And as you start to change!"

There was a PIFF! PAFF! POOF!
And an ALAKAZOOM!
Tiny little crackles!
And a scary big BOOM!

Everything went quiet
"Why don't you take a look?"
He checked his reflection
In a little close brook

What he saw surprised him
He gasped "But can it be?
That wolf in the water,
That wolf there! Is that me?!"

"That's right!" Said the fairy
"I made your dream come
true!
That wolf that you see there
Is not a dream, it's you!

But you have to be careful
And listen to me well
Should someone touch your
tail
That will break the spell!"

14

The fox was so happy
He jumped around with glee
He let out a big howl
"ARROOOOO! FINALLY!"

His big howl was so loud
It bounced all through the trees
It frightened all the birds
It worried all the bees

A pack of wolves came by
To see who'd made the sound
That was so big and loud
It rumbled through the ground!

"What a howl you have there!
So loud! So proud! So strong!
You should join in our pack
Come on and join our song!"

The fox was delighted
He'd waited for this day
To have a pack of wolves
to learn their wolfy ways!

They ran through the forest
They played and they had fun
They howled in the moonlight
They slept when there was sun

But for our little friend
His body felt quite strange
Everything was different
Since his body had changed

He wasn't so nimble
He wasn't quite so fast
His body wasn't light
Like it was in the past

18

One bright and clear full moon
When the wolves were at play
The fox felt he was slow
He couldn't run away

He tried to run quite fast
But he felt like a snail
And a wolf cub caught him
And bit him on the tail

There was a flash of light
There was a great big roar
And then there stood a fox
Where a wolf was before

All the wolves were surprised
This was a magic spell?
They thought he was a wolf
As far as they could tell!

"That's right I was a fox
I'm sorry that I lied
I wished to be a wolf!"
The little red fox cried

"But Fox you are perfect
We find it very strange
We love you as you are
Why would you want to change?

Your body is so small
Why would you want to grow?
You're faster than we are
Our bodies make us slow!

You don't need to worry
This doesn't have to end
You can still play with us
You'll always be our friend!"

Now when the moon is full
And you hear the wolves howl
Close your eyes and listen
For that proud fox's yowl

Our fox learned a lesson
There's no need to pretend
You can just be yourself
And you will make real friends

Printed in Great Britain
by Amazon

84416978R00016